For Pat and Veronica Coles
—JC

For Ashlyn and Aeva
—CD

The Wishing of

Biddy Malone

story *by* JOY COWLEY

illustrated by CHRISTOPHER DENISE

PHILOMEL BOOKS

To be sure, Biddy Malone loved to sing and dance. But her singing was like a rusty gate in a wild west wind, and when she danced, her great dundering feet fell over each other, which was terrible considering Biddy Malone always wanted the best for herself. So whenever she made a mistake, she kicked and screamed something awful, her temper being a fine fierce thing.

Her brothers teased her. They rattled their spoons on the table and chanted, "Shuffle and moan. Shuffle and moan. That's the dancing of Biddy Malone."

One fine afternoon, she got fired up like a baker's oven. She threw a whole pan full of milk at those brothers and stamped out, slamming the door near off its hinges. Along the street she ran, out of the village and down to the river.

Oh, but there was no slowing those angry legs. Strong they were, making their own path to a place far beyond gardens and the quiet breath of cattle. When they stopped at last, Biddy was looking all about her at a strangeness.

Now, it was the soft hour between day and night, when shadows played games with the eyes. But what Biddy saw down by the river was no shadow. Settled between the trees were little houses. There were sparkling lights at the windows and a music so lovely, it fair melted her bones.

To be sure, it was a faerie village, the kind that children were warned about. Never, never go near the little people, parents said. But all that went clean out of the head of Biddy Malone. The music had hold of her and her feet danced across the grass, not once arguing with each other.

Now, Biddy was mortal high and the houses faerie small, but by the time she got there, she was exactly the right size for the doorway that led to the music. In she went to a sight that filled her with happiness and just a pinch of fear. The place was crowded with little folk, singing and dancing in fine style. The women wore dresses of poppy petals and corn silk. The men had eyes the color of the river and sky, and hair that fell in their faces as they kicked up their heels.

Now, when the little folk saw Biddy Malone, the music
stopped, the dancing stilled, and the whole room went quiet as
sleep. One by one, the faerie people moved back against the wall
and Biddy saw, at the far end of the hall, a most beautiful boy
with skin like an acorn and hair as soft as midnight. A loveling he
was, with a band of meadow flowers about his head, a cloak of
grouse feathers at his shoulders, and silver rings on all his fingers.

"I've been waiting for you, Biddy Malone," he said.

He walked toward her and his fine smile wrapped itself around her. "It is three wishes you are wanting," he said.

Three wishes? Biddy stared at him.

His dark eyes seemed to go on forever. "Are you able to name them, Biddy Malone?"

Biddy swallowed. "I . . . I didn't come here for wishes. But to be sure, now that you mention it, there are two great yearnings. I would like to sing as sweetly as a thrush and dance as lightly as a deer."

"You will do both those things," the boy said.

A sweet tinkling laughter broke out in the room and the little folk whispered to each other.

He clapped for silence. "Wishes always come in threes," he said.

She took a deep breath and let it out with a sigh. "I'm minded there is something else. I've got a temper like a steaming kettle and it does nobody any good. I am wishing for a loving heart."

He smiled, his eyes full of light. "It is yours," he said. "Now, Biddy Malone, let us dance."

The music began again. The boy took Biddy's hands in his and twirled her across the floor. Her feet were so light, she felt she was flying. Her heart beat a single note of pure happiness. All around the room, the faerie folk swayed as flowers in a summer breeze and sang in tiny voices. Biddy sang, too. Her voice came back to float around her ears like strands of a beautiful silver thread as she danced and danced.

To be sure, Biddy did not want it to end at all. But end it did, and suddenly. The boy stopped the dancing. The music died.

"Time to go now, Biddy Malone," he said, kissing her on the forehead.

Her heart fluttered. "No!" she cried. "I've only just arrived."

He shook his head slowly and led her to the door. In a moment, she was outside on the darkened riverbank, the wind blowing her hair. She turned to say good-bye, but the loveling was not behind her. Neither was the doorway, nor the house. Indeed, the whole faerie village was gone, and there were only the dark shapes of willow trees amongst the reeds.

Biddy knew that this was the way of the little people, here one moment, gone the next. She walked back to her house, and there, in the light of the porch, she saw a strange thing. A large black ribbon hung on the door, the kind that folk hung out when they were in mourning.

All of her family was at the table. When they saw her, her brothers stared with great round eyes and her mother screamed and fell back in her chair. Her father, his face as white as bread dough, leaned across the table. "We thought you were dead!"

"Dead? Dadda, I've only been away half an hour!"

"Two months!" cried her eldest brother. "You walked out of here two whole months ago. We had your wake and all."

"Where did you disappear to, girl?" shouted her father.

"Half an hour!" insisted Biddy. But already she was noticing changes in the room, a new pot on the stove, her brothers and father in different shirts.

"Two months!" bellowed her father, thumping the table.

Her mother grabbed her father's arm. "She's been with the little people," she said in a voice full of fear.

A few days later, Biddy Malone told her mother about the faerie village by the river. But she was not doing any talking about the beautiful boy and the three wishes.

To tell the truth, they were not working, those wishes. She still sang like a squeaking gate and danced with feet like bricks. The difference was the faerie music that echoed inside her, giving her legs and voice a kind of knowing. Every day she danced for hours. Little by little, her singing got better, her feet lighter.

As for her temper, it improved as well. Her mouth could still get terrible fierce at times, but she would whisper to herself, "Loving heart, loving heart," and then, surprisingly, she would go all adreaming of the beautiful loveling of the little people.

For weeks her mother worried about her. "Biddy, little folk are full of trickery. Once they get a hold of you, you know, they don't let you go."

But after a time of seeing that her daughter was happier and kinder than ever before, she hushed her fretting.

With no help at all from the wishes, Biddy went on singing and dancing. She made her own magic from the faerie music within her, until her voice was oh so pure and her feet oh so nimble that her performance was something to behold. Before long, the people in the village were asking her to sing and dance for them.

"Our Biddy was late in flowering," said her father. "But now she's got a voice like a songbird and she's as light on her feet as a deer."

The truth it was. But Biddy was still not satisfied. She continued to work hard at her wishes and it so happened that by the time she was a full-grown woman, she was the best singer and dancer in the country.

Sure, and a big loving heart had grown in her. But there was a problem about that. Although she was fond of people, Biddy Malone could not fall in love. Her singing and dancing brought young men from near and far. With shining eyes and gifts in their hands, they came seeking her favor.

"Will you come acourting, acourting, acourting? Will you come acourting, sweet Biddy Malone?" they sang.

Biddy was kind to all of them, but she would not choose any for a husband, for that space in her heart was still filled with the loveling. How she longed for him! Many a time she went down to the river, hoping to find the faerie village. It was never there. So, beneath all that success, she had a sadness as deep as a well.

When she walked in the garden, the thrushes on the bean fence sang, "Biddy Malone, all alone," and when she was in the forest, picking berries, the deer would toss their heads and heels. Biddy Malone, all alone. Biddy Malone, all alone.

Biddy was tired of the longing and loneliness. What was the use of moping like a sick hen for something she couldn't have? One evening, she said to her family, "The next time a good man asks me to marry him, I will most definitely say yes."

Well, you know, late the following day, there came a knocking at the door. It was the young schoolteacher from the village. He had a bunch of flowers in one hand and a speckled trout wrapped in paper in the other. "Will you marry me, Biddy Malone?" he asked.

"Say yes," whispered her mother.

"Say yes," said her father.

Her brothers stood behind her and nudged her back. "Say yes! Say yes! Say yes!"

Biddy tried, but for the life of her, the yes would not come out. All she could see in her heart was a beautiful boy with hair as soft as midnight and eyes that went on forever.

"Will you marry me?" the schoolteacher asked again.

Biddy's lips were locked tight. But as she stood there, she heard a sound coming up from the river, faerie music made thin by distance.

Without a word, she pushed past the teacher and slammed the gate. It was not pleasure she was feeling. Indeed, no. As she walked through the village, the last bit of temper in her flared and cracked like a brush fire. She swung her arms. She tossed her head. Oh, but she was fine and fierce by the time she got to the river.

She knew it would be there, the little village amongst the willows. To be sure, it was, and looking the same with houses of twisted tree roots, roofs of dried grass. There were lights in the windows and the music she knew as well as she knew herself. Ignoring the sweetness of the sound, she marched so fast to the open door that the rush of her shook the reeds along the riverbank.

Inside, the little people were waiting, the beautiful boy in front of them, his hands outstretched. "Biddy Malone!" he called.

Biddy was too fired up to notice his smile. "Faerie trickery and foolery!" she shouted. "You lied to me!" Her anger created a whirling wind that blew the petals clean off the flowers in his hair. All around the room, silken dresses and shirts flapped like flags.

"Those wishes were useless!" she yelled.

The boy laughed in a shower of little petals.

She screamed at him. "Worse than useless! First of all, the singing and dancing. Oh, I got there all right, but I had to do the work myself."

He came closer. "Biddy, hushathee a moment!"

But Biddy would not be hushed. "The third wish!" she cried, her voice tasting of tears. "It worked, did the third wish. But you tell me! What's the use of a loving heart if it can't have what it loves most in the whole world?"

He put a finger across her lips. "Biddy, mavourneen, listen! I didn't offer to grant you your wishes. I just asked you to name them. Then I told you they would be yours. Something gained for nothing has no value."

Biddy stopped to think. To be sure, if her talents had been given to her for nothing, they would have been worth just that. It was all her hard work that had made her singing and dancing her own.

The boy went on, "As for love, dear Biddy, I've been carrying your image in my heart since the beginning of time. Wisha! I have and all! But I needed to wait until you were sure. Yestereen your head told you to take a husband. But your heart loved me so well that it would not let you marry another. I knew then that the time was right and I could come back for you."

Biddy didn't know what to say. As the deep space in her heart filled with the light of his loving, the storm of her anger faded. The room became calm and the faerie folk set about straightening their coats and dresses.

"I am yours, Biddy Malone," he said.

She smiled and sighed and smiled again. Sure now, she was not over good at love talk, but there was a song fine and ready inside her and her feet were twitching like grasshoppers' legs.

Her loveling held out his hands. "Welcome home, Biddy Malone. Let us dance."

PATRICIA LEE GAUCH, EDITOR

Published simultaneously in Canada.   Manufactured in China by South China Printing Co. Ltd.
Designed by Semadar Megged.   Text set in 15.75-point Fournier.   The artwork was created with acrylic
paint and charcoal on gessoed illustration board.

Library of Congress Cataloging-in-Publication Data
Cowley, Joy. The wishing of Biddy Malone / Joy Cowley ; illustrated by Christopher Denise. p. cm.
Summary: In Ireland, a young girl who cannot sing, dance, or control her temper stumbles across a faerie
village, where a beautiful boy asks her to name her three wishes—but does not promise to grant them for her.
[1. Wishes—Fiction. 2. Self-actualization (Psychology)—Fiction. 3. Fairies—Fiction. 4. Ireland—Fiction.]
I. Denise, Christopher, ill. II. Title.
PZ7.C8375 Whe 2004   [Fic]—dc21   2002155693
ISBN 0-399-23404-7
1 3 5 7 9 10 8 6 4 2
First Impression